# FAVOURITE
# IRISH
# Legends
# Colouring
# Book

Gill Books

# Contents

# Fionn *and the* **Dragon**

Fionn set off on the road to Tara. It was busy with people arriving for the great festival of Samhain. Fionn arrived in time for the feast but there was no seat for him in the banqueting hall. The High King did not recognise him.

"I am Fionn, the son of Cumhall," he declared.

There was silence and all eyes were on Goll Mac Morna, the man who had killed Fionn's father, Cumhall. Then the king spoke.

"You are welcome to my feast."

During the feast the High King told Fionn of an evil spirit in the form of a fire-breathing dragon which had been preying upon the people of Tara. Many warriors and magicians had tried and failed to slay it.

"What reward will be given to the man who can rid you of the dragon?" Fionn asked.

"Anything he wants," replied the king.

"In that case I will defend Tara from the evil spirit," said Fionn.

Fionn walked to the outer walls of the city. The people were gathered safely inside the walls. Suddenly a man appeared.

"I was a friend of your father's and I have come to repay a favour your father did for me. When the dragon approaches he plays sweet music. Anyone who hears this music falls asleep at once. Take this magic spear and as soon as the music begins press it against your forehead and the music will have no power over you."

From the darkness came a low, sweet sound.
It was the magic music of the Fairyworld.
Immediately Fionn put the spear to his forehead
and, although the people of Tara fell into a deep
sleep, Fionn remained awake.

The dragon suddenly appeared before Fionn, breathing a long blue flame. Fionn took aim, raised his arm and fired the spear straight at the dragon, which fell dead on the spot. Fionn cut off the dragon's head.

"What is your wish?" the High King asked.

"To be leader of the Fianna as my father was," replied the proud hero. The High King agreed.

"You have a choice to make," the High King said to Goll Mac Morna. "You can accept Fionn as

your leader or you must leave Ireland." Goll thought for a while and then spoke to Fionn.

"Here is my hand. I will gladly serve you."

So Fionn became their leader, as his father before him had been.

## The *Fairy Lios*

One afternoon in early summer, Eithne and her brother Connor were playing in the field behind their house. Eithne was busy making daisy chains and then she decided to pick some of the wild flowers that were growing in the field.

"Don't pick the flowers from the fairy lios, Eithne, or you will be sorry," Connor warned. Eithne ignored him. "There are so many growing here that the fairies couldn't possibly notice if a few were picked," she answered.

The children returned home and Eithne put the flowers in a vase. When their mother heard that she had picked them from the lios, she rushed outside and put them on the window ledge. She knew that if the fairy people were angry

Eithne might be punished. And so she was! When Eithne lay down in bed that night she jumped up screaming. Her bed was full of nettles! She tried Connor's bed but the same thing happened.

"I'm sorry I ever went near the lios," she cried.

Her parents went to visit a wise old woman who lived nearby to ask what they should do.

"If someone in your family could do a good deed for the fairies, perhaps they might remove the nettles," she said.

Connor had an idea. At midnight, he crept out of the house and went to the lios. He could hear soft, light music. Connor loved music and he could play all sorts of tunes on his feadóg (tin whistle). He recognised some of these tunes.

He pulled back the bushes to see the fairies and leprechauns dancing merrily!

When the music stopped Connor crept forward. One of the leprechauns spoke angrily.

"Your sister disturbed our lios and now you!"

"No, no," said Connor. "I have come to tell you how sorry she is. Please take the nettles from her bed and let her sleep."

"Impossible!" said the leprechaun. He turned to the musician. "Let the music start again!"

Connor stood outside the lios feeling sad. His sister would never again sleep in a bed. Then he had an idea. He began to play a soft, sad tune. He parted the bushes and stepped into the lios. This time the fairy people listened.

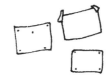

When he finished, the applause began and the leprechaun who had spoken earlier spoke again.

"Well played, Connor. We must reward you."

"Oh no, I don't want anything for myself. I just want help for my sister Eithne."

The leprechaun nodded. "Return home," he said. "I will grant your wish."

Dawn broke and instantly the lios was empty. Connor returned home to find Eithne fast asleep in bed. He had broken the spell!

# Paddy and the Phouka

Paddy loved stories about phoukas, who played jokes on people. They could be fierce and frightening, or kind and helpful.
One day, Paddy felt an odd wind – it must be a phouka, going to where the fairies danced!

"Phouka," he called out. "Let me see you!"
Suddenly a bull charged at Paddy! He threw his
coat on the bull, which stopped and said,

"Go to the mill tonight when the moon is full,
and you'll have good luck!"

That night, Paddy went to the mill. There were sacks of corn lying around, but the men who worked there were asleep. Paddy was tired and went to sleep too. When he awoke, the corn had all been ground into flour, even though all

the men were still sleeping soundly. For several nights the same thing happened. Paddy decided he must stay awake and see how the corn was ground! So he crept into an old chest in the mill with a big keyhole that he could peep out of.

That night, he spied six little men, each carrying a sack of corn. They were followed by an old man in ragged clothes. The little people set to work, and soon all the corn was ground. Paddy knew the old man was the phouka he had met.

In the morning, Paddy told his father what he had seen. "Let the phouka work," his father said, "but I will sack my lazy men." Paddy's father soon became very rich, but he never spoke of the phouka, for that would bring bad luck.

Paddy often hid in the chest to watch the phoukas. He was sad that the old man, who worked so hard, only had tattered rags to wear. So he saved up his pocket money until he had enough to buy a splendid suit of clothes which would keep the phouka warm in the cold mill. One night, before climbing into the chest, he laid the clothes out on the floor. When the old fairy came in, he was amazed.

"For me?" he cried. "I shall be a fine gentleman."

The phouka put the suit on and paraded about. He looked at the corn, waiting to be ground.

"No more work for me!" he cried. "I'm a gentleman now, too grand to grind corn!"

He kicked his old rags into the corner and

disappeared into the darkness. No corn was ground ever again by the phoukas. But Paddy's father was rich – and when Paddy got married, a gold cup, full of wine, appeared on his table. Paddy knew it was a present from the phouka.

# The *Salmon* of Knowledge

Long ago in Ireland the king had an army of soldiers called the Fianna to guard him. Cumhall was their most famous leader, but his jealous enemies killed him. Cumhall's wife was afraid that her son Fionn might also be killed.

So she took him to two women warriors who lived in the Sliabh Bloom Mountains. She asked the women to teach the young boy all that a son of Cumhall should know, for she knew that one day her son would become one of the Fianna.

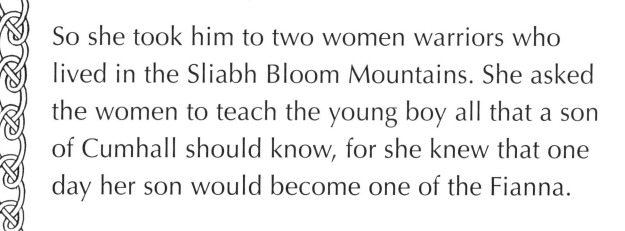

At that time, any youth wishing to join the Fianna had to pass very difficult tests. He had to defend himself against the spears of nine men using only a shield; he had to jump over a pole as high as his head; and he had to recite twelve books of poetry. When the women had taught

Fionn all the fighting skills he would need, they sent him to Finnéigeas the poet to learn the twelve books of poetry. Finnéigeas had lived for many years on the banks of the river Boyne, fishing in its waters.

There was a fish in the Boyne known as the Salmon of Knowledge. The person who ate it would know all there was to know in the world. One day, Finnéigeas caught a large salmon.

"Cook it for me, Fionn, but you must not eat it."

Fionn did as he was told. He cleaned the salmon, lit the fire and put the salmon over the fire to cook. All was well until a blister rose on the side of the salmon. Without thinking, Fionn reached out and broke the skin of the blister.

In doing so he burnt his thumb and sucked it to stop the pain. He finished cooking the fish as Finnéigeas returned. The old man looked at Fionn and saw in his eyes the knowledge he had spent so many years searching for.

"There is nothing for me to teach you now," he said sadly. "You must go to Tara and take your father's place at the head of the Fianna."

After that, whenever Fionn had a problem, he put his thumb in his mouth to find the answer.

# The Beggarman

"This will be a good day," said Conán Maol. "Today I will run faster than anyone!"

Everyone laughed, because Conán was short and rather fat. Suddenly, a voice said:

"You, run fast? Rubbish! No-one can outrun me."

With that, a strange-looking sight appeared. An old beggarman dressed in a long, tattered coat stood before them. On his feet he wore enormous boots that were so caked with mud that he could barely lift his feet to walk.

Meanwhile a ship had sailed into the bay, and a warrior jumped ashore. The Fianna were taken by surprise.

The warrior pointed to the Fianna and declared,

"I offer a challenge. Choose your swiftest runner

to race against me. The winner shall have the gold, horses and chariots of Eire."

"Caoilte Mac Rónáin is our fastest runner," replied Fionn, "but he is away in Tara."

"We must race now!" cried the warrior.

The beggarman immediately stepped forward to accept the challenge. "If Fionn will give us two horses, I suggest that we ride sixty miles today and race back tomorrow."

The Fianna were stunned.

Early next morning, the warrior woke the beggarman to begin the race.

"I would never dream of running this early. You set off and I will follow you later," said the beggarman and, curling up, he fell asleep.

When he awoke he set off after the warrior, jumping and hopping, but never running and soon he had overtaken him. The bushes were thick with juicy blackberries and the beggarman stopped to gobble them up. When the warrior

caught up, the beggar was covered in juice.

"Your coat tails are caught in a bush ten miles back," snarled the warrior, racing past.

The beggarman ran backwards, found them, and with three long hops caught up with the warrior.

The Fianna cheered as the race was won by the beggarman. The warrior raised his sword in anger but suddenly the warrior's head was rolling on the ground. The beggarman threw it back on the warrior's shoulders back to front!

The Fianna realised that the beggarman was, in fact, the prince from Tír na n-Óg, who once a year became human.

And, as he waved farewell, the beggarman changed into a tall fair-haired prince.

# Soul Cages

One day Jack Dogherty met a merrow, sitting on the the rocks near Jack's home.

"Good day to you, Jack," the merrow called. "Your grandfather was a great friend of mine. We often enjoyed a drink together."

"How do you get drink under the sea?" asked Jack. "I thought it was all salt water."

"There are barrels and bottles in ships that sink," the merrow said. "Why don't you meet me here tomorrow, and I'll take you to my house!"

The next day Jack went out to the rocks again. The merrow was there, holding two red hats.

"Put this on, jump in and hold my tail," he said.

Down they went through the water, until they got to a flat, dry, sandy area. In front of them

was a pretty cottage, and a meal awaited them. Over dinner, washed down with delicious things out of the merrow's enormous collection of bottles, Jack learned that the merrow's name was Coomara, but usually he was called Coo.

Jack asked Coo about the rows of wicker cages like lobster pots stacked against the walls.

"Oh, those are soul cages," Coo told him. "I put them out when there's a storm at sea. The souls of drowned fishermen and sailors creep

into them, and then I bring them home to keep them dry." Jack peered into a cage near him. He couldn't see anything, but he could hear the sound of crying. He felt sorry for the caged souls, who should be on their way to Heaven.

Back home, Jack thought hard about what he could do for the trapped souls and worked out a plan. Next day, he invited Coo to his house. Jack collected bottles that were washed up on the beach after storms and shipwrecks.

That evening, when Coo came, Jack had built up a good fire so the cabin was warm. He gave Coo some very old, strong brandy. He poured Coo another, and another, and soon the old merrow fell fast asleep by the fire.

Quickly, Jack took Coo's red hat, ran to the rocks, and leapt into the sea. At Coo's house he collected all the soul cages and took them outside. As he opened each one there was a tiny flicker and a faint whistle.

When every one was empty, Jack put them back where he'd found them. He went home to find Coo still asleep by the fire. To Jack's surprise, Coo never noticed that his soul cages had been emptied!

# Deirdre of the Sorrows

When the baby Deirdre was born, her father, Feidhlim, asked the wise druids what the future held for her. The druids answered: "She will grow up to be the most beautiful girl in Ulster, but she will cause many deaths."

When the Red Branch Knights of Ulster heard this they went to King Connor demanding that Deirdre be killed. The king had a solution:

"Deirdre will be brought up far away from here and when she is old enough I will marry her."

Deirdre was taken away at once to a deep wood. The king chose a wise old woman called Leabharcham to care for her. As Deirdre grew older she became as beautiful as the druids had foretold, with golden hair and deep blue eyes.

But she was a very lonely girl.

One day, Deirdre told Leabharcham about a dream she had every night.

"I dream of a tall warrior, with raven black hair and snow white skin. He is fearless in battle."

"He is Naoise, one of the Sons of Uisneach. You must never mention your dream again. You will be married to King Connor very soon," said Leabharcham. But Deirdre begged her to send for Naoise and finally Leabharcham gave in.

Deirdre and Naoise met and fell in love. They knew they must leave Ulster at once. Deirdre, Naoise and his brothers travelled all around Ireland but everyone was afraid to help them. Finally they sailed to a small Scottish island.

There they lived for some time until one day a messenger arrived from the king. He reported that King Connor had forgiven them.

Deirdre did not trust the message but the Sons of Uisneach believed it. Reluctantly, Deirdre set off

with them to Ireland. She pleaded with them to turn back but they would not listen.

When they arrived they were sent to the house of the Red Branch Knights, not the king's castle. Now Deirdre was sure that a trap had been set!

Deirdre was right. The Sons of Uisneach were seized and brought before Connor, who demanded they be killed.

Suddenly an unknown warrior stepped forward and cut off the heads of the Sons of Uisneach.

Deirdre screamed and fell dying to the ground, heartbroken. Deirdre's father was so angry that he left Ulster for Connacht, taking many warriors with him, to join the army of Queen Maeve.

So Deirdre did bring sorrow to Ulster as foretold.

# Niamh

Niamh sat up in bed and listened carefully. She could hear strange sounds and decided to investigate. She slipped on her dressing gown and made her way to the bedroom door.

Down the stairs she crept.

It was difficult to see because the only light to guide her was the light of the full moon that shone through the window.

As she reached the kitchen door she knew that she was not alone. It was her brother Liam.

"Where are you going?" he whispered.

"I heard music and I'm going to find out who is playing it. You can come with me," she replied, "but only if you do what I tell you."

The children stood outside in the moonlight

and listened. The music seemed no more than a rustling of leaves. Was it the fairy people their grandmother had told them about?

They decided to follow the path to the clearing in the wood and set off into the chilly night.

A faint light flickered as they approached the clearing and they could hear music. To Niamh, it seemed as if the music was calling her.

"Not too close," Liam warned. "Gran said that if the fairy people catch you, they'll keep you."

Niamh crept closer and closer to the light and Liam peeped through the branches. What a sight it was! Lights twinkled from the trees in the clearing. The children could see little people dancing in the centre – leprechauns!

A new dance began with a faster rhythm. The music seemed to call them to join in. Liam remembered Gran's warning to cover his ears.

Niamh was spellbound. She began to move in time with the music. Suddenly there was a flash

of light and Liam was blinded for a moment. When he opened his eyes again, he was alone and his sister had vanished. The search for Niamh went on for a long time but there was not a trace of her to be found.

One day, many years later, Liam returned to the clearing in the wood. He visited the spot where his sister had disappeared whenever he could. As he approached he heard a child calling,

"Liam! Where are you? We must go home."

A little girl ran up to him and asked,

"Have you seen my brother? We were dancing for twenty minutes and now he's wandered off!"

"Niamh," said Liam, "You weren't just twenty minutes, you were gone for twenty years!"

# *Setanta*

**S**etanta wanted to become one of the famous Red Branch Knights of Ulster. His father had told him about the special school, the Macra, for boys who would one day join the brave warriors. Setanta pleaded with his parents to let him go.

"You are much too young, Setanta," they said. But Setanta could wait no longer. One day he set off for the Macra. On the way Setanta had his hurley and sliotar to play with. He hit the sliotar far ahead and ran to catch it on his hurley stick.

89

When Setanta reached the castle of King Connor at Armagh, he found the boys of the Macra were playing hurling and he hurried over to join in. Almost at once he scored a brilliant goal.

Furious at the stranger, the boys attacked him.

Setanta was brought before the king.

"I am Setanta, your nephew. I have come to join the Macra because I want to become one of the Red Branch Knights."

The king liked Setanta and welcomed him.

Time passed quickly for Setanta. He loved his new life at the Macra.

One day, Culann, the blacksmith who made spears and swords for Connor invited the king, his knights and Setanta to a feast.

Setanta was playing a game of hurling, so he told the king that he would follow later. The feast began but Connor forgot to mention Setanta's late arrival. Thinking everyone had arrived, the blacksmith unchained his guard dog.

When Setanta arrived at Culann's house the hound leapt forward out of the dark to attack. With all his strength Setanta hurled his sliotar down the hound's throat. He caught the animal by its hind legs and dashed it against a rock.

The wolfhound fell down, dead. Inside, the feast party had heard the dog growling.

"I forgot about Setanta!" Connor cried.

He and the Red Branch Knights rushed out expecting to find the young boy torn to pieces.

Connor was amazed and delighted to find his nephew alive and he was proud of his great strength. Culann was relieved that the boy was safe but he was sad that he had lost the wolfhound he loved, which had faithfully guarded his house every night.

"Let me take the place of your hound until I have trained one of its puppies," said Setanta.

From that day on Setanta was called Cú Chulainn, which means the Hound of Culann.

# The New House

The twins were very excited when they heard that they were moving to a new house. Now that the children were getting bigger, the cottage seemed too small for all the family. The children were delighted to hear that their Granny would

be coming to live in their old home.

"That means that we will see her every day," said Ronan.

The children loved their Granny and they especially loved to hear her stories.

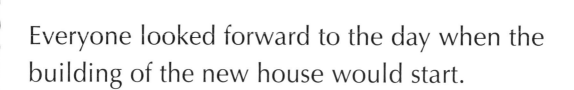

Everyone looked forward to the day when the building of the new house would start.

One day Granny came to visit. The children told her of their plans and all was well until Granny asked where the new house was to be built.

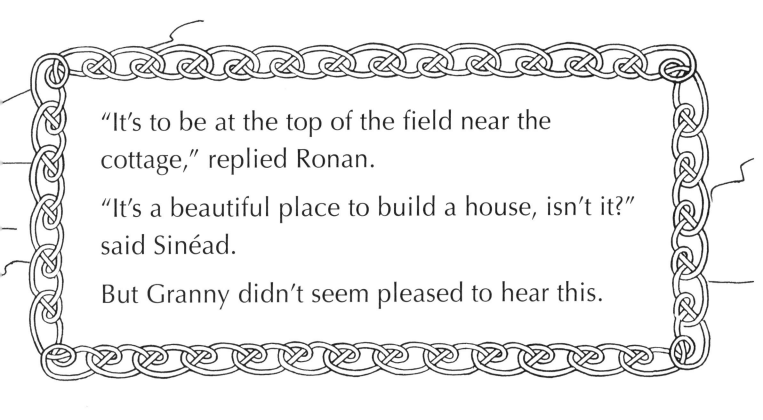

"It's to be at the top of the field near the cottage," replied Ronan.

"It's a beautiful place to build a house, isn't it?" said Sinéad.

But Granny didn't seem pleased to hear this.

Granny hurried to speak to the children's father.

"Eamon," she said, "you can't build your new house at the top of that field. The fairy people live there. No one must ever disturb them. If you do, you will never again have any luck!"

Eamon refused to listen to her.

"No one believes stories like that any more!"

The building began. Every night the children talked and planned excitedly, but they noticed that Granny never joined in the conversations.

On the day the family moved into the new house, Eamon held a big party to celebrate. It was a beautiful summer's evening. Eamon had organised musicians and both young and old joined in the dancing.

At midnight, a breeze began to stir and soon it got stronger and colder until it became a howling wind. The sky grew darker with huge black clouds. Suddenly, strange hammering noises came from inside the roof.

One by one the guests left. By now the noises were much louder and they seemed to come from everywhere – the roof, walls and chimney. The children were terrified.

"It's the fairies and leprechauns!" they cried. Granny was right.

"We must go quickly, right now!" she cried. Eamon was the last to leave. He looked back and gasped! He could hear leprechauns hammering and smashing!

The house shuddered and collapsed. Then the little people disappeared in a swirl of leaves.

Eamon and his family lived for many years in their little cottage. No one ever dared to touch the pile of bricks that had been their new house.

As time went by, the site of the new house became overgrown with hawthorn bushes and wild flowers and the land at the top of the field belonged once again to the fairy people.

So wise old Granny had been right all along.

# Oisín in Tír na n-Óg

One morning the Fianna were hunting deer on the shores of Loch Léin in Kerry. They saw a beautiful woman on a white horse coming towards them. She wore a long blue dress, and her shiny golden hair hung to her waist.

"What is your name and what land have you come from?" asked Fionn, Leader of the Fianna.

"I am Niamh of the golden hair. My father is king of Tír na n-Óg," she replied. "I have come to find a brave warrior called Oisín."

Oisín was the son of Fionn, a hero and a poet.

"Tell me," Oisín asked Niamh, "what sort of a land is Tír na n-Óg?"

"Tír na n-Óg is the land of youth," she replied. "It is a happy place, with no pain or sorrow. Any

wish you make comes true and no one grows old there. If you come with me you will see."

Oisín mounted Niamh's horse and they galloped off over the water. As they left, Oisín promised to return soon.

Oisín was welcomed in Tír na n-Óg. It was a wonderful land, just as Niamh had said. He hunted and feasted and told stories of Fionn and the Fianna and of their lives in Ireland.

Before long Oisín and Niamh were married.

One day Oisín decided to visit his home.

"Take my white horse." said Niamh. "But, whatever happens, you must not get off the horse and touch the soil of Ireland. If you do you will never again return to me or to Tír na n-Óg."

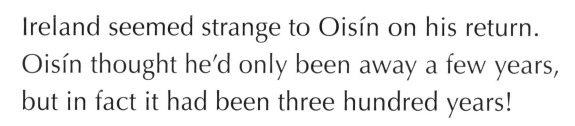

Ireland seemed strange to Oisín on his return.
Oisín thought he'd only been away a few years,
but in fact it had been three hundred years!

There was no trace of his father or the Fianna.
The people he saw seemed small and weak.

As he rode on he saw some men trying to move a large stone, and offered to help. The men were terrified of the giant! Stooping from his saddle, Oisín lifted the stone. With that, the saddle girth broke and Oisín was flung to the ground.

Immediately the white horse disappeared and the people saw before them an old, old man.

Suddenly Oisín remembered Niamh's warning not to touch the soil of Ireland. "Where is my father and the Fianna?" he asked.

When he was told that they were long dead he was heartbroken. He spoke of the adventures of Fionn and the Fianna and of his time in Tír na n-Óg with his beautiful wife. Although he died soon after, the stories of Oisín have lived on.

# The *Sidhe*

Séan lived in a cottage near a small village. During the long winter nights the villagers met to tell stories or sing to pass the time.

Unlike his neighbours, Séan didn't believe in fairies or leprechauns or any of the little people.

In fact, whenever he heard anyone talk about the Sidhe he would laugh and say that he couldn't understand how anyone could be so foolish as to believe that such stories could possibly be true.

The Sidhe

One warm summer day, Séan was resting by the edge of his field. The air was filled with various sounds. He heard birds chirping and busy bees humming as they collected pollen.

Suddenly, he became aware of another sound.

It was a gentle tap-tapping coming from a nearby hedge. Séan hurried to investigate.

There before him sat a leprechaun! He was sitting on a mushroom working hard. At his feet lay lots of tiny pairs of shoes and boots.

In a flash, Séan reached out and grabbed him.
"Where is your pot of gold?" he demanded.

"Gold!" said the little man crossly. "Where
would I get gold? I'm only a poor shoemaker.
All I have are my tools and this piece of leather."

"You can't fool me," said Séan. "Give me your gold and I'll set you free."

"All right!" the little man cried.

"My gold is buried safely in the field by the river. Take me there and I'll show you."

Séan knew that he must not take his eyes off the leprechaun for an instant. The leprechaun led him to a bush by a stream.

"There you are," he cried. "Take my gold."

Keeping his eyes on the little leprechaun, Séan

reached into the bush. Suddenly he screamed in pain, for instead of a pot of gold it was a bee hive! Séan looked to see where the bees were, but the moment Séan took his eyes off the leprechaun the little man vanished.

It was just as everyone had said in their stories on those long winter evenings.

Séan never told anyone how the leprechaun had fooled him when it was his turn to tell a story during the long, cold winter nights.

But one thing was certain – no-one ever again heard Séan say that he didn't believe in fairies or leprechauns or little people!

# The *Magic Cloak*

It was almost dawn. Both sea and land were covered in mist. Eoin hid behind the rock as the tide ebbed far out into the bay. He had been waiting a long time for this day. Every seven years a very strange magical event happened.

The sea went out as far as the horizon and the fairy people appeared. They spread a magic cloak on the sands to hold back the tide. The owner of the cloak could order the sea to stay back and make good fertile land for a farm.

Seven years earlier, Eoin had watched in amazement as the waves rolled back and the fairy people appeared! This time he waited with his horse. At dawn Eoin heard the music of the fiddles and harps.

Through the mist Eoin could barely make out
the shadows. The mist lifted and once again
Eoin saw the strangest sight before his eyes. The
sea and sand had disappeared and in its place
was a green plain as far as he could see.

If Eoin got the magic cloak the land would be his! But the cloak was guarded by leprechauns. He soon spotted them sitting in a circle, a pile of tiny shoes at their feet, tapping in time to the music. They were sitting on the cloak and the

edges were flapping in the breeze. Eoin pulled gently on the reins of his horse as they moved forwards. It took him longer than he expected to reach the cloak. When he looked back, it seemed that the shoreline was very far away.

As he came nearer the leprechauns he slowed his horse and then dismounted a short distance away. He crept forward. He thought that they must hear his heart thumping or the sound of his breathing but no, they continued to work.

He reached out and grabbing a corner of the cloak he pulled it from under them. He threw the cloak on his back, mounted his horse and galloped towards the shore. He could hear the chaos behind him but he dared not look back.

Suddenly all was quiet. Then Eoin heard a rumbling noise. He looked over his shoulder to see a gigantic wave moving towards him. It was the Fairy Wave! Eoin urged his horse on but he was swept from the saddle. As quickly as it had

come the wave disappeared. When Eoin woke, every bone in his body ached.

"I've survived the Fairy Wave," he thought. "I have the magic cloak and I'll be rich."

But instead all Eoin had was a cloak of seaweed.

# Lazy Annie and her Amazing Aunts

Annie was very beautiful. She was also very, very lazy! One day a prince rode by her house and heard Annie's mother scolding her.

"Surely you aren't scolding that lovely girl?" The woman couldn't admit how lazy Annie was.

"My daughter works too hard! She can spin, weave and make shirts within three days."

"My mother is the best spinner in the land," said the prince. "I'd like to take Annie home with me and introduce her to the queen!"

The old woman still couldn't admit that Annie was so idle, so she agreed to let her daughter go. Annie rode off with the prince and on the journey they fell in love. But still Annie didn't confess that she couldn't spin, weave or sew!

At the castle, the queen welcomed Annie,
delighted to hear what a hard worker she was.
That night, the queen left a huge pile of flax in
Annie's room and asked her to spin it into thread
by the following day.

Annie began to cry. Suddenly, an old woman with huge feet appeared!

"Ask Colliach Cushmor to your wedding, and the thread will be ready tomorrow," she said.

Annie agreed and by morning the flax was spun

into the finest thread. The queen was delighted.

"Tomorrow you can weave that into cloth." But Annie couldn't use a loom! As she sat sobbing an old woman with huge hips appeared.

Colliach Cromanmor offered to weave the thread

in exchange for a wedding invitation. That evening, the queen admired the cloth.

"You can make it into shirts tomorrow," she said.

Next morning, as Annie sat crying, a third old woman arrived. She had an enormous red nose!

She was Colliach Shrón Mór Rua, and in return for a wedding invitation, she made the shirts.

When Colliach Cushmor came to the wedding the queen asked why she had such huge feet!

"Because I've stood spinning all my life."

"Annie, never spin again," cried the prince.

When Colliach Cromanmor arrived the queen demanded to know why her hips were so huge. "Because I've sat at a loom all my life,"

"Never weave again," the prince told Annie.

Then the old woman with the red nose told them it was due to her bending over sewing every day.

"Dearest, never sew!" cried the prince.

So, thanks to the old fairies, Annie never had to spin, weave, or sew, but lived a long and idle life!

# Children *of* Lir

Once upon a time there lived a king called Lir who had four children: a daughter named Fionnuala and three sons called Aodh, Fiachra and Con. Their mother the queen was dead, and the children missed her terribly. The king saw that

his children needed a mother, so he married again. His new bride, Aoife, was beautiful, but she was jealous of the children because their father loved them so much. So she asked a druid to help her to get rid of them with an evil spell.

One day while the children played at the lake, Aoife pulled out a magic wand and waved it. In a flash the children vanished and were replaced by four beautiful white swans.

"I have put a spell on you," declared Aoife.

"You will be swans for 900 years. You will spend 300 years on this lake, 300 years on the Sea of Moyle and 300 years on the Isle of Glora. Only the sound of a church bell can break the spell."

When the children did not return home that evening the king went to search for them. As he came to the lake four swans swam up to him.

"Father," they cried, "we are your children. Aoife has placed a terrible magic spell on us."

The king pleaded with Aoife to reverse the spell but she refused and he banished her from the kingdom. Nobody knew how to break the spell.

Lir stayed by the lake, with his children, until he grew old and died. The swans were heartbroken.

After 300 years the swans moved to the cold and stormy Sea of Moyle. They were tossed about by the wild waves and dashed against sharp rocks. It was a harsh life and the years passed slowly. When the time came for them to fly to the Isle

of Glora, the swans were old and tired. Although it was warmer on the island and there was lots of food, they were still very lonely.

Then one day they heard the sound they had waited for. It was the sound of a church bell.

The bell was ringing in the tower of a little church. An old man, called Caomhóg, stood outside. He was amazed to hear swans talking and listened to their sad story in astonishment. Then he went inside his church and brought out some holy water which he sprinkled on the swans while he prayed.

As soon as the water touched them, the swans miraculously began to change into an old, old woman and three old, old men.

Caomhóg told them about God's love. Fionnuala put her arms around her brothers and they fell to the ground, dead. That night Caomhóg dreamed he saw four swans flying up through the clouds – the children of Lir were on their way to Heaven.